Little Miss Helpful set about organising the party.

But as you may, or may not, know Little Miss Helpful is not as helpful as her name would suggest.

For, as hard as Little Miss Helpful tries to be helpful the more unhelpful she becomes.

She tried to sort out the bunting, but somehow or other she only made things worse.

LITTLE MISS PRINCESS
AND THE Very Special Party

Roger Hargreaves

Original concept by
Roger Hargreaves

Written and illustrated by
Adam Hargreaves

EGMONT

Little Miss Helpful had heard it was a very special occasion.

It was a Royal occasion.

A Royal occasion that called for a big party.

A very big party.

The sort of party that would fill a whole street.

A street party.

And Little Miss Princess would be the guest of honour!

She tried to make the party food, but somehow or other the jam ended up in the ham sandwiches and the mustard on the cream scones.

Ham and jam sandwiches and mustard cream scones ...

YUCK!

Little Miss Helpful was in a panic.

Everything was going wrong and it had to be perfect for Little Miss Princess.

"Hello, what's the matter?" said a voice behind her.

It was Little Miss Naughty.

So Little Miss Helpful explained.

"That's easy to solve, just let me help you," suggested Little Miss Naughty, and she smiled.

The sort of smile that you might have seen a crocodile smile.

A smile that meant trouble.

But it seemed to Little Miss Helpful that for once Little Miss Naughty was being very good and helpful.

She arranged for Mr Tickle to hang the bunting.

She persuaded Mr Strong to arrange the tables.

She got Mr Impossible to sort out the weather.

And she drew up a plan of where everyone was going to sit.

The day of the party arrived and Little Miss Helpful was very pleased with all the work that had been done.

Soon everyone started to arrive and take their seats at the long table that ran the whole length of the street.

It was then that Little Miss Naughty smiled that particular smile again. Do you remember?

The crocodile smile.

And why?

Because it was then it started.

The quarrelling.

The arguing.

The squabbling.

For you see, Little Miss Naughty had carefully seated each person next to someone they would not get along with.

She had seated Mr Messy next to Little Miss Neat. Mr Mean next to Mr Uppity. Little Miss Chatterbox next to Mr Quiet. Mr Clumsy next to Mr Fussy. And poor Little Miss Shy next to Mr Rude!

It was a disaster! There was lots of shouting and somebody threw a cream scone.

Little Miss Helpful did not know what to do. The guest of honour, Little Miss Princess, was about to arrive at any moment.

It was then that Little Miss Helpful had a brainwave.

"STOP!" she yelled at the top of her voice. "It's time for a game of musical chairs!"

The music started and the guests danced around the table. When the music stopped everyone dived for the nearest chair.

Little Miss Neat found she was sitting next to Mr Fussy, Mr Messy was beside Mr Clumsy, Little Miss Chatterbox was next to Mr Noisy. Mr Uppity was next to Mr Rude. And Little Miss Shy found that she was next to Mr Quiet.

Suddenly everyone was happy!

And just in time!

Because at that moment Little Miss Princess arrived
to a fanfare of trumpets.

The party had changed in an instant!

Everyone was having a wonderful time.

The time of their lives!

Everyone, that is, except for Little Miss Naughty.

Little Miss Helpful had one more job for her ...

... the washing up!